The Gingerbread Man

Retold by Jim Aylesworth

Illustrated by Barbara McClintock

SCHOLASTIC INC.
New York Toronto London Auckland Sydney

ISBN 0-439-05772-8

Text copyright © 1998 by Jim Aylesworth.
Illustrations copyright © 1998 by Barbara McClintock.
All rights reserved. Published by Scholastic Inc.
SCHOLASTIC and associated logos are trademarks and/or registered trademarks
of Scholastic Inc.

12 11 10 9 8 7 6 5 4 3 2 1   8 9/9 0 1 2 3/0

Printed in the U.S.A.   14
First Scholastic paperback printing, May 1998

Book design by David Saylor
The text type was set in 14-point Edwardian Medium.
The display type was hand lettered by Chris Costello.
The artwork was rendered in watercolor, sepia ink, and gouache.

To Dianne Hess, with love!
— J. A.

To Larson, Dianne, and David
— B. M.

Once upon a time,

there was a little old man and a little old woman.

One day, the little old woman said, "Let's make a gingerbread man!"
"Yes, let's do!" said the little old man, and they did.

So, they mixed up the batter,

and they rolled out the dough,

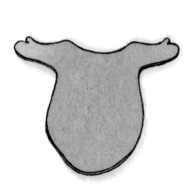

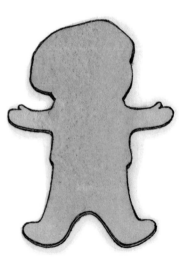

and they shaped
the little arms,

and they shaped
the little legs,

and they shaped
the little head.

And with raisins, they made the little eyes and the little nose and the little mouth, and then with sugar glaze, they dressed him in a fancy suit of clothes.

When all was set, they put the gingerbread man into the oven, and they waited.

Pretty soon, a delicious smell coming from the oven told them that the gingerbread man was ready, and so were they!

But when they opened the oven door, out popped the
Gingerbread Man, and he ran across the floor.

The little old man and the little old woman could hardly believe their eyes! The Gingerbread Man looked up at them, put his little hands on his hips, and said,

"Run! Run!
Fast as you can!
You can't catch me!
I'm the Gingerbread Man!"

The little old man reached down to grab him, but quick as a
wink, the Gingerbread Man ran out the door and down the road,
and the little old man and the little old woman ran after him.

"**Come back! Come back!**" they yelled. But the Gingerbread
Man just looked over his shoulder, and said,

"No! No!
I won't come back!
I'd rather run
Than be your snack!"

And he kept on running.

And he ran,

and he ran,

and he ran,

and after a time, he met a butcher standing in front of his shop.
The Gingerbread Man looked up at him, put his little hands on
his hips, and said,

"Run! Run!
Fast as you can!
You can't catch me!
I'm the Gingerbread Man!
I've run from a husband!
I've run from a wife!
And I'll run from you, too!
I can! I can!"

The butcher reached down to grab him, but quick as a wink, the Gingerbread Man ran on down the road, and the butcher ran after him!

"**Come back!**" yelled the butcher.

And not far behind, the little old man and the little old woman were yelling, too! "**Come back! Come back!**"

But the Gingerbread Man just looked over his shoulder, and said,

"No! No!
I won't come back!
I'd rather run
Than be your snack!"

And he kept on running! And he ran, and he ran, and he ran.

And after a time he met a black-and-white cow. The Gingerbread Man looked up at her, put his little hands on his hips, and said,

"Run! Run!
Fast as you can!
You can't catch me!
I'm the Gingerbread Man!
I've run from a husband!
I've run from a wife!
I've run from a butcher
With a carving knife!
And I'll run from you, too!
I can! I can!"

The black-and-white cow reached out to grab him. But quick as a wink, the Gingerbread Man ran on down the road, and the black-and-white cow ran after him!

"**Come back!**" yelled the black-and-white cow.

And not far behind, the little old man, and the little old woman, and the butcher with the knife were yelling, too!

"**Come back! Come back! Come back!**"

But the Gingerbread Man just looked over his shoulder, and said,

"No! No!
**I won't come back!
I'd rather run
Than be your snack!**"

And he kept on running. And he ran, and he ran, and he ran.

And after a time, he met a muddy old sow.

The Gingerbread Man looked up at her, put his little hands on his hips, and said,

"Run! Run!
Fast as you can!
You can't catch me!
I'm the Gingerbread Man!
I've run from a husband!
I've run from a wife!
I've run from a butcher
With a carving knife!
I've run from a cow
All black and white!
And I'll run from you, too!
I can! I can!"

The muddy old sow reached out to grab him. But quick as a wink, the Gingerbread Man ran on down the road, and the muddy old sow ran after him!

"**Come back!**" yelled the muddy old sow.

And not far behind, the little old man, and the little old woman, and the butcher with the knife, and the black-and-white cow were yelling, too!

"**Come back! Come back! Come back! Come back!**"

But the Gingerbread Man just looked over his shoulder, and said,

"No! No!
I won't come back!
I'd rather run
Than be your snack!"

And he kept on running.

And he ran,

and he ran,

and he ran.

And after a time, he met a fox. The Gingerbread Man looked at him, put his little hands on his hips, and said,

"Run! Run!
Fast as you can!
You can't catch me!
I'm the Gingerbread Man!
I've run from a husband!
I've run from a wife!
I've run from a butcher
With a carving knife!
I've run from a cow,
And a muddy old sow,
And I'll run from you, too!
I can! I can!"

"What did you say?" asked the fox. The tricky fox pretended that he couldn't hear well. "I'm not as young as I used to be," he said. "You'll have to come closer and speak louder."

The Gingerbread Man stepped closer, and in a very loud voice, he said,

"Run! Run!
Fast as you can!
You can't catch me!
I'm the Gingerbread Man!
I've run from a husband!
I've run from a wife!
I've run from a butcher
With a carving knife!
I've run from a cow,
And a muddy old sow!
And I'll run from you, too!
I can! I can!"

Just then, the little old man, and the little old woman, and the
butcher with the knife, and the black-and-white cow, and the muddy
old sow came running around a turn in the road! And they were yelling!
"Come back! Come back! Come back! Come back! Come back!"

The Gingerbread Man looked over his shoulder,
but before he could say a single word, the fox
jumped up and grabbed him!

And quick as a wink,
Before he could think,
With a snap and a snick,
And a lap and a lick,
The Gingerbread Man
Was gone!

The little old man, and the little old woman, and the butcher with the knife, and the black-and-white cow, and the muddy old sow all stood and stared sadly at the fox. He hadn't left a single crumb for anyone.

Riddle-riddle ran, fiddle-fiddle fan,
So ends the tale of the Gingerbread Man.